POEMS FOR BROTHERS,
POEMS FOR SISTERS

POEMS FOR BROTHERS.
POEMS FOR SISTERS

selected by *Myra Cohn Livingston*

illustrated by *Jean Zallinger*

Holiday House/New York

Text copyright © 1991 by Myra Cohn Livingston
Illustrations copyright © 1991 by Jean Zallinger
All rights reserved
Printed in the United States of America
First Edition

Library of Congress Cataloging-in-Publication Data
Poems for brothers, poems for sisters / selected by Myra Cohn
Livingston : illustrated by Jean Zallinger. — 1st ed.
p.   cm.
Summary: A collection of poems exploring the relationship
between brothers and sisters, by authors including X. J. Kennedy,
Lewis Carroll, and Ted Hughes.
ISBN 0-8234-0861-2
1. Brothers and sisters—Juvenile poetry.   2. Children's poetry,
American.   3. Children's poetry, English.   [1. Brothers and
sisters—Poetry.   2. American poetry—Collections.   3. English
poetry—Collections.]   I. Livingston, Myra Cohn.   II. Zallinger,
Jean, ill.
PS595.P76P64   1991   90-44463   CIP   AC
811.008′0352045—dc20
ISBN 0-8234-0861-2

CONTENTS

THE DOLL

I told her she was my sister
and she told me her name
Sophronia Destiny
and how the others
sometimes called her Dusty
because she had lived
a very long time in an attic.
When I found her there
her eyes were wide
and blue as summer
her plump arms lifted
and we hugged ourselves
together for always
my sister and me.

JULIA CUNNINGHAM

THE ONLY CHILD

In this small town
I am the only only child I know,
the only ten-year-old spy
with a nose pressed flat against
cold kitchen windows.

Better than a movie—families
at dinner. At every mouthful
something collides—an elbow, a shoulder.
You jostle, shout! Quarrels
fly out to me where I crouch in the dark.

Mornings we walk to school.
Ours is the house with nothing broken.
Snow lies smooth as the sheet
pulled up to my chin. I dress, I knock
at your doors.

"Your friend is here,"
your mother calls. No one suspects
my disguise or how each day I pretend
that I live in your houses.
Each day we cut through yards
where snow is trampled by many sisters,
many brothers.

RUTH ROSTON

LITTLE

I am the sister of him
    And he is my brother.
He is too little for us
    To talk to each other.

So every morning I show him
    My doll and my book;
But every morning he still is
    Too little to look.

Dorothy Aldis

8

HE MAKES ME *SO* MAD

I nail my
little brother
with a stare

where he sits
at the counter
giving me

his smart mouth
while I boil my
egg. Beyond

him, Father
simmers in his
easy chair,

our four heads
lining up: Dad,
daughter, son,

and hard-boiled
egg hot-headed
in its cup.

JOHN RIDLAND

BATH

My sister and I are pushing a big aluminum tub
across our brick patio to the grass.
We sound like a tank rolling toward war.

I hold the hose. She turns the spigot.
Water thunders into the tub like a drum roll
filling it up.

Searching,
we find Peanuts trembling behind bushes,
camouflaged.

His head down,
his paws gripping the passing grass,
we pull him across the yard.

I drop down
to rub his nose.

Then, my sister,
because she is older,
lifts him into the tub.

APRIL HALPRIN WAYLAND

MY BROTHER LOVES SMALL ANIMALS

My brother loves small animals,
especially birds.
Three times he brought home
baby swallows and nursed them.
He placed them in a shoebox
half-filled with cotton
and fed them milk with a water dropper.
He would gently move the wings
(to keep the muscles lively).
A few times I would help,
but it was hard
because I had to be
so careful with the
baby birds—and I
am so small myself.

EMANUEL DI PASQUALE

12

REFLECTIONS

My brother, my braggart,
you gave our sister a Christmas prism
which whirls and twirls in her room
and dances and catches her fancy
and fetches her eye with hues
and lights and shapes that slide
along its glass surface, like you.

BETSY HEARNE

13

14

RHINOS PURPLE, HIPPOS GREEN

My sister says
I shouldn't color
Rhinos purple,
Hippos green.
She says
I shouldn't be so stupid;
Those are things
She's never seen.
But I don't care
What my sister says,
I don't care
What my sister's seen.
I will color
What I want to—
Rhinos purple,
Hippos green.

MICHAEL PATRICK HEARN

SISTER HAS A BLISTER

Sister has a blister.
She looks like something hot
Came up to her and kissed her.
Did she sip from a pot

Of blazing cocoa? No, sir,
That blister simply rose.
I sort of love my sister
But that thing really shows.

X. J. KENNEDY

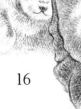

SOUPS AND JUICES

Did you hear about my big brother?
The lucky stiff is sick.
All day they bring him soups and juices.
When he calls, they come running.
They keep puffing his pillow.

I'm supposed to stay out
but tonight I peeked in.
He was asleep.
The dumb kid
kicked off his blankets
so I went and covered him up.
He looked *small*.

RICHARD MARGOLIS

BROTHER AND SISTER

"Sister, sister, go to bed!
Go and rest your weary head."
Thus the prudent brother said.

"Do you want a battered hide,
Or scratches to your face applied?"
Thus his sister calm replied.

"Sister, do not raise my wrath.
I'd make you into mutton broth
As easily as kill a moth!"

The sister raised her beaming eye
And looked on him indignantly
And sternly answered, "Only try!"

Off to the cook he quickly ran.
"Dear Cook, please lend a frying-pan
To me as quickly as you can."

"And wherefore should I lend it you?"
"The reason, Cook, is plain to view.
I wish to make an Irish stew."

"What meat is in that stew to go?"
      "My sister'll be the contents!"
                        "Oh!"
"You'll lend the pan to me, Cook?"
                              "No!"
Moral: Never stew your sister.

Lewis Carroll

SORRY

Hair-tousled sorry
in his floppy blue bathrobe
      my brother came to me
      just before I fell asleep
sparkled stars around me
      my big brother
      in his blue bathrobe

EMILIE GLEN

MY BROTHER

I used to think
how good it would be
if I was the onliest
kid in this house.
But when you went to camp,
I was the loneliest.

BOBBI KATZ

SUNDAY NIGHT ORANGES

One Sunday night, my brother
brought home a thousand oranges
in a burlap sack. As my mother
held me on her lap,
he spilled the oranges
all over the kitchen floor.
We all laughed—
so many oranges.
He ate some oranges
skin and all.
I remember orange
bits hanging from
his moustache.

EMANUEL DI PASQUALE

24

SISTERS

When Nan and I were little
we sometimes used to fight:
she'd read my secret diary
and I would scratch and bite.

If she pulled up the window shade
I would want it down;
if she wore short pajamas
I'd wear a long nightgown.

But then we learned it's better
to have a sister-friend,
someone beside you in the dark,
someone to hold your hand.

Now we're glad my hair is long
and hers is short and curled.
The difference doesn't matter:
we're two against the world.

RUTH WHITMAN

ALL MY HATS

All my hats
are hats he wore.
What a bore.

All my pants
are pants he ripped.
What a gyp.

All my books
are books he read.
What a head.

All my fights
are fights he fought.
What a thought.

All my steps
are steps he tried.
What a guide.

All my teachers
call me by my brother's name.
What a shame.

RICHARD MARGOLIS

27

MY SISTER JANE

And I say nothing—no, not a word
About our Jane. Haven't you heard?
She's a bird, a bird, a bird, a bird.
Oh it never would do to let folks know
My sister's nothing but a great big crow.

Each day (we daren't send her to school)
She pulls on stockings of thick blue wool
To make her pin crow legs look right,
Then fits a wig of curls on tight,
And dark spectacles—a huge pair
To cover her very crowy stare.
Oh it never would do to let folks know
My sister's nothing but a great big crow.

When visitors come she sits upright
(With her wings and her tail tucked out of sight).
They think her queer but extremely polite.
Then when the visitors have gone
She whips out her wings and with her wig on
Whirls through the house at the height of your head—
Duck, duck, or she'll knock you dead.
Oh it never would do to let folks know
My sister's nothing but a great big crow.

At meals whatever she sees she'll stab it—
Because she's a crow and that's a crow habit.
My mother says "Jane! Your manners! Please!"
Then she'll sit quietly on the cheese,
Or play the piano nicely by dancing on the keys—
Oh it never would do to let folks know
My sister's nothing but a great big crow.

TED HUGHES

29

SKATING IN THE WIND

I crouched.
My brother Bill shoved hard.
I held up my jacket;
the wind caught it, shaped it taut like a sail.

The wind slammed into my back.

My skates clattered.
Skidding,
Skimming,
like butter in a hot skillet.

Mouth dry,
the wind roared in my ears.

Bill said I was almost flying

Until the fence.

Kristine O'Connell George

31

ACKNOWLEDGMENTS

Grateful acknowledgment is made to the following poets, whose work was especially commissioned for this book:

Julia Cunningham for "The Doll." Copyright © 1991 by Julia Cunningham.

Emanuel di Pasquale for "My Brother Loves Small Animals" and "Sunday Night Oranges." Copyright © 1991 by Emanuel di Pasquale.

Kristine O'Connell George for "Skating in the Wind." Copyright © 1991 by Kristine O'Connell George.

Emilie Glen for "Sorry." Copyright © 1991 by Emilie Glen.

Bobbi Katz for "My Brother." Copyright © 1991 by Bobbi Katz.

John Ridland for "He Makes Me *So* Mad." Copyright © 1991 by John Ridland.

Ruth Roston for "The Only Child." Copyright © 1991 by Ruth Roston.

April Halprin Wayland for "Bath." Copyright © 1991 by April Halprin Wayland.

Ruth Whitman for "Sisters." Copyright © 1991 by Ruth Whitman.

Grateful acknowledgment is made for the following reprints:

Faber and Faber Ltd. for "My Sister Jane" from *Meet My Folks* by Ted Hughes. Reprinted by permission of Faber and Faber Ltd.

Macmillan Publishing Company for "Reflections" from *Love Lines* by Betsy Hearne. Copyright © 1987 by Betsy Hearne; for "Sister Has a Blister" by X.J. Kennedy from *Ghastlies, Goops & Pincushions*. Copyright © 1989 by X.J. Kennedy. Reprinted with permission of Margaret K. McElderry Books, an imprint of Macmillan Publishing Company; for "All My Hats" and "Soups and Juices" by Richard J. Margolis from *Secrets of a Small Brother*. Copyright © 1984 by Richard J. Margolis. Reprinted with permission of Macmillan Publishing Company.

McIntosh and Otis, Inc. for "Rhinos Purple, Hippos Green" by Michael Patrick Hearn from *Breakfast, Books & Dreams*. Copyright © 1981 by Michael Patrick Hearn. Reprinted by permission of McIntosh and Otis, Inc.

The Putnam Publishing Group for "Little" by Dorothy Aldis from *Everything and Anything*. Copyright © 1925–1927, copyright renewed 1953–1955 by Dorothy Aldis. Reprinted by permission of G.P. Putnam's Sons.